one careless night

christina booth

For my brother Paul,

and all who believe.

WALKER BOOKS
AND SUBSIDIARIES
LONDON • BOSTON • SYDNEY • AUCKLAND

Where the mist
swallows mountains
and wild winds whisper
through ancient trees,
myths and legends are born.
There are forests here
where no one has trod
and creatures run free in
endless rain and deep, dark bush.

Here lives a mother with her pup.
When night devours the sun, they hunt.
As wallabies graze in the dying light,
they stalk, silently choosing their prey.

She shows her how to survive.

They hear the crack of a whip
echo from the mountain face.
It is swallowed by the river.

The blast of gunpowder
breaks through the ancient land.

They run from this creature
that searches for them.
They hide deep in the bush
in the belly of an ancient pine.

The rain settles softly,
the smell of earth and pine
comforts them,

it hides the scent of wet leather and old meat.

The trap has been laid.

Caught.
Carted away.
Sold for a bounty.

Locked away in a forest
of concrete and steel,
her mother grows tired
and fades
like mist in the sun.

Only she remains.

Alone.

She paces,

waiting for the food they bring her.

No longer can she remember the hunt
or the soft wind that carries the scent
of ferns and pine.

She forgets she is tyger.

Her stripes echo the bars of her cage.

She plays with her keeper,
dances on concrete
and sings to the sun.

Back and forth she paces until she is old.

Her calls grow silent, for no tyger can answer.

In the cold of one careless night,

she is gone.

Now, furs that were trophies
hang in shame.
Memories flicker to life in the dark
and glass-eyed tygers stand faded,
forever on display.
Some say they have seen them.
Some continue to search.

Today,

the mist still swallows mountains

and winds whisper

through ancient trees

as creatures run wild and free.

Listen.

In the dying sun and shroud of night

she still sings to her kin.

Like a ghost in the night, there is a flash

of stripe on sandy fur

and then, it is gone.

Can you hear?

Did you see?

Or was it a trick of

the moonlight?

author's note

The last known living thylacine was called Benjamin. There are conflicting accounts as to whether Benjamin was male or female. In *One Careless Night* the author has chosen to make the last thylacine a female.

Benjamin died one freezing night at the Hobart Zoo because her keeper left her out of her shelter. Many other animals also died that night from lack of care, and Benjamin's body, along with the others, was reported to have been disposed of at the city rubbish tip.

Benjamin, the last thylacine in captivity, died on 7 September 1936. This is now the date of National Threatened Species Day in Australia.

Reward for Destruction of Native Tigers.

154. A reward of One Pound shall be payable out of the Consolidated Revenue for the destruction of every full-grown Native Tiger (*Thylacinus cynocephalus*), and the sum of Ten Shillings for every half-grown or young Native Tiger, subject to the following conditions.

155. The person claiming such reward, or person authorised in writing by him, shall produce to the proper officer the skin of the animal complete, with head (or scalp) and paws adhering thereto, and shall satisfy the said officer that the said animal was captured and destroyed.

156. Any one of the following officers is hereby authorised to certify to the destruction of Native Tigers, and upon his certificate the amount of reward shall be paid:—

The Secretary for Lands,
A Stipendiary Magistrate,
A Warden of a Municipality,
A Police Clerk,
A Council Clerk,
A Superintendent of Police, and
A sub-Inspector of Police.

157. Upon the production of a skin so complete as aforesaid to any such officer, he shall make a round hole therein immediately behind the forearm, not less than half an inch in diameter, and the skin so mutilated shall become the property of the person claiming the reward.

158. The officer to whom the claim for reward is made shall declare upon the voucher for payment as follows:—

> I hereby certify that .... has satisfied me that .... has destroyed * .... Native Tiger... the complete skin... of which ha...... been produced to me, and that I have mutilated the same, according to law.

159. On and after the day on which these Regulations shall come into force, no reward shall be paid for the production of a tiger skin unless the same shall be produced in a complete condition, as hereinbefore provided.

160. All claims for rewards for the destruction of Tigers, together with voucher for payment, duly signed and certified to, are to be forwarded to the Secretary for Lands, Hobart.

First published in 2019 by
Walker Books Australia Pty Ltd
Locked Bag 22, Newtown
NSW 2042 Australia
www.walkerbooks.com.au

This edition published in 2021

EU Authorized Representative: HackettFlynn Ltd.,
36 Cloch Choirneal, Balrothery,Co. Dublin, K32 C942, Ireland.
EU@walkerpublishinggroup.com

A catalogue record for this book is available from the National Library of Australia

ISBN 978 1 760653 95 8

Every attempt has been made to contact the copyright holder of the bounty notice shown on the previous page. The publisher would be pleased to hear any further information regarding copyright of this document.

The illustrations for this book were created digitally.
Typeset in Carrotflower
Printed and bound in China

10 9 8 7 6 5 4 3 2